W9-AAV-604

more titles in
The Secret Games of Maximus Todd!

Frantic Friend Countdown

Max has a dilemma. Everyone's got a best friend except him. But when a new kid arrives at the school, Max plays a secret game to make him Max's buddy. Too bad the new kid would rather hang out with barf-breath Mandy Beth, peskiest pest in the entire town!

Big Game Jitters

It's the soccer championship and Max's team is playing the school bully's team. Of course, as soon as the match starts, Max's gets a case of the Super Fidgets. If Max can't invent a secret game to calm them, it might cost his team the championship.

Flu Shot Fidgets

Max is at the doctor's office, where the stress of getting a needle sets off his Super Fidgets. Quick-thinking Max invents a secret game to try to stay calm. But Max will have to invite #1 pest, Mandy Beth, over for a play date if he loses.

Hyper to the m

by L. M. Nicodemo

illustrated by Graham Ross

Formac Publishing Company Limited
Halifax

Formac Publishing Company Limited recognizes the support of the Province
of Nova Scotia through Film and Creative Industries Nova Scotia. We
are pleased to work in partnership with the Province of Nova Scotia to
develop and promote our creative industries for the benefit of all Nova
Scotians. We acknowledge the support of the Canada Council for the
Arts which last year invested $157 million to bring the arts to Canadians
throughout the country.

Cover design: Meghan Collins
Cover image: Graham Ross

Library and Archives Canada Cataloguing in Publication

Nicodemo, L. M., author
        Hyper to the max / L.M. Nicodemo ; illustrated by Graham Ross.

(The secret games of Maximus Todd)
ISBN 978-1-4595-0419-6 (hardback)

        I. Ross, Graham, 1962-, illustrator II. Title.

PS8627.I245H96 2016   jC813'.6   C2015-907248-4

Formac Publishing Company Limited   Distributed in the United States by:
5502 Atlantic Street   Lerner Publishing Group
Halifax, Nova Scotia, Canada   1251 Washington Ave N
B3H 1G4   Minneapolis, MN, USA
www.formac.ca   55401

Printed and bound in Canada.

Manufactured by Friesens Corporation in Altona, Manitoba, Canada in
May 2016.

Job #222748

For all the kids who have had

ONE OF THOSE

days!

Contents

Chapter One

A Case of the super fidgets

Maximus Todd woke with a sudden jolt early one Monday morning. His heart was thump-thumping. His legs were wiggling. And his arms felt all prickly, right down to his fingertips.

Inside Max's head was a RUCKUS.
"Oh no," he moaned. "It's going
to be one of THOSE days!"
THOSE days were when Max
could not keep still.

FIDGETY. JITTERY.

BOUNCING OFF THE WALLS.

On weekends or during summer
holidays it was no big deal. But
when it happened on a school
day — THAT was a real disaster.
After all, what kid could stay out
of trouble if he was as jumpy as
popcorn in a **MICROWAVE?**

GOOD THING MAX WAS CLEVER.

He knew how to make his Super Fidgets not so super. *He'd invent a game to play in his head.* By keeping busy on the inside, he would be less hyper on the outside.

Max put his hand under his chin and tried to think.

"NOW ALL i need is an idea," He said.

By the time Max's mom came into his room, Max was dressed for school. He started humming the song from his favourite show, *Cyborgs of Justice*.

"Da, daaa dum dum." It was his good-mood hum. He felt a lot better.

"Wow, you sure got ready early," Mom said, giving him a hug. "How about some cereal and toast?"

Max thought for a couple of seconds.

"Um . . . i'D LiKe THaT THe *MOST*."

His mother laughed. "You are
easy to please, my guy."

She headed down the hall to
get Sarah. Max could hear his
baby sister yelling from her crib,
"Up, up, up!"

"Thanks, Mom. I really try," he
called after her.

At breakfast, Max used **TWO**
spoons to eat his Cocoa Laser
Beams cereal. He wanted to be

quick — quicker than Granpops,
who was at the other end of the
table reading his newspaper.

On most mornings, Max's
grandfather kept pretty quiet.
"Won't get a peep out of me till I've
had my coffee!" he'd say. Today
that was exactly what Max wanted.
Before Granpops finished his one
cup, Max hoped to be done his
whole breakfast. Done and gone.

But the clanking spoons caught his grandfather's attention. "Hey, buddy. Take it easy," he said to Max. "You're eating too fast."

Max looked up from an almost empty bowl. He tried to hide one of the spoons under a napkin.

"WELL, IT'S HARD TO MAKE IT . . . LAST," HE SAID.

His grandfather grumbled, but returned to his paper.

Max went back to using two spoons. Only this time, no clinking and clanking. Once the cereal was gone, *so was Max*.

Chapter Two

The
Game

Back in his room, Max went through a morning checklist. He always did stuff in the same order every day. If he didn't, he'd feel all wonky inside, like a puzzle with missing pieces.

- ☑ SCHOOL BAG PACKED
- ☑ TEETH BRUSHED
- ◯ HAIR COMBED

Max stared in the
mirror and frowned.
He patted his hair.
He pushed his hair.
He spit on his hand
and tried to smooth
his hair down.

NO
DIFFERENCE. IT
SPRANG RIGHT
BACK UP.

Max shrugged.
*Hair combed —
check.*

Now he thought
about his game.

He Had Sworn an Oath.

Judges on television made people do that all the time. Max knew it meant that what he said counted for real.

"I, Maximus Todd, promise that whenever someone talks to me I will rhyme back. I have to rhyme until the final bell at school.

And if i lose, i will give away all my Laserman comics. The end."

Max glanced over at his comic book collection. The comics were stacked neatly on the shelf. Plastic baggies protected each one. He pulled out issue #18 — *Laserman Battles Destructo* — and gave it a hug.

Losing this game would be the most terrible thing in the world, **worse than broccoli.**

It was now time to go. Max opened the door of his bedroom. He peeked out into the hallway, making sure it was empty. No point in talking to people unless he had to.

"COAST CLEAR," Max whispered,

sounding like a spy. "Time to get out of here."

He FLeW DOWn THe STaiRS.

At the front landing, he threw on his runners, snatched his jacket and made a dash for the door. Suddenly, something grabbed at his backpack. He glanced behind. It was his mother.

Max gasped. If there was

one thing he knew about his mom, it was that she always had something to say.

"My guy!" Mom said. "Not so fast! Where's my kiss?"

Aha! Like I figured, Max thought. He looked up into his mother's smiling face and then smiled back. "How could I forget . . . *this*?" he said.

He pressed a mushy smooch on her cheek and raced outside.

Chapter Three

Escaping the world's
BIGGEST PEST

Phew! That was close, thought Max once he reached the sidewalk. Now if I can get to school before —

A SHOVE AT MAX'S BACK ALMOST MADE HIM TRIP.

"GOOD MORNING, MAX," SAID MANDY BETH IN A SING-SONG, SNOOTY VOICE.

She swung her long ponytail and swiped Max on the side of his head. **On purpose.**

Max scowled.

He had exactly three complaints about Mandy Beth Bokely. And they were doozies.

1. She lived only a couple doors down from HIS house.
2. She was in HIS grade three class at Rosewood Elementary.
3. She was the world's biggest pest. EVER.

"Hi," Max mumbled back,

walking a bit faster. He pulled at his ear lobe. "Uh . . . my ear has too much wax."

Mandy Beth wrinkled her nose in disgust. *Good*, thought Max.

"Remember we get to see a movie today, Max? I hope it's not boring. Ms. Rudy said it'll be about plants," Mandy Beth said all in a rush.

"It should be okay," said Max. "At least it's not about . . . ants." He kicked at a stone and stretched out his steps even more.

FROWNING, MANDY BETH HURRIED TO KEEP UP.

"What do ants have to do with it?"

Max felt his heart bump-thump hard in his chest as he worked to come up with a rhyme.

"GEESH, MANDY BETH, DO I HAVE TO EXPLAIN EVERYTHING?" HE GRIPED.

"Ants aren't as cool as plants. Okay? **Not one bit.**"

Now Max was walking so fast that Mandy Beth had to jog to keep up. **He pretended not to see the puzzled look on her face.**

"Hey! What's going on here?" she demanded, grabbing at his arm.

MAX BLINKED HARD. "NOTHING . . . UMM . . . UH . . ." HE FORCED OUT A RHYME.

"MY DEAR."

Instantly, Max's cheeks went pizza-sauce red. He made an extra ugly face, the kind that he usually gave behind Mandy Beth's back.

THEN HE SET OFF RUNNING.

Chapter Four

QUICK Thinking

BRRRING! Max slipped in through the classroom door just as the bell rang. Kids were already at their desks, excited for the school day to begin. As he scrambled down his row, he noticed Mandy Beth.

SHE WAS GRINNING AT HIM LIKE A CAT — A CAT THAT HAD TRAPPED A MOUSE.

It made Max feel uneasy.

"Maximus Todd! You were almost late," his teacher said.

"Sorry, Ms. Rudy. That wouldn't be great." Quickly he went to his desk.

The national anthem played. Max stood and sang along. He could feel his Super Fidgets itching to bust out so he wiggled his toes from inside his runners. Wiggle-waggle. Wiggle-waggle.

IT BARELY HELPED.

He needed to play his game.

Even so, would he be able to rhyme the whole day?

It was too late to change the rules now.

After announcements, Max went with his math group to work on a multiplication poster.

They were making a forest
scene about the number eight.
Everybody got busy — except
Max. He sunk low in his chair,
kicked his legs up and down
under the table and **waited for
someone to say something.**

Lori Skenders was the first
to bug him. She was the leader

of the group, mostly because she liked telling people what to do. She poked at Max's arm. "Can you cut out leaves for the trees?"

"Sure," he said, sitting up. **"Um . . . Pass the scissors . . .** *please.*" Max was surprised at how quickly he had made a rhyme!

Lori reached for a pair of scissors. But she didn't hand them over.

"Let me SHOW you," she said, like Max had never cut paper before. "Do it this way." She moved the scissors along a traced leaf.

"Uh . . . okay," Max nodded. Two for two!

He cut carefully as Lori watched over his shoulder.

"Looks like you know what you're doing," she finally told him in her usual snippy voice.

"Uh huh!" said Max. "And it's more fun than . . . **GLUING.**"

At the far end of the room,

Mandy Beth's group was drawing jars of candy on their poster. While she coloured in jellybeans, Mandy Beth looked over at Max.

"Time to cause some trouble," she muttered under her breath.

She got up and crossed over to Max's table.

"Hey, Max, do you have an extra blue MARKER?" The way Mandy Beth raised her voice when she said "marker" told Max that she had somehow discovered what he was doing.

What a *pain*, he thought, wishing Mandy Beth didn't know about his secret games.

She had forced it out of him
a while ago, after kidnapping
his Laserman figurine. "Tell me
a secret," she had said to him,

"and I will give it back." Max
had first refused. But when she
threatened to kiss Laserman
right on the face, he gave in
and told her everything.

"NOBODY ELSE KNOWS,"

he had explained, making
her spit-swear to never say
anything to anyone. Ever.

But then she'd asked if
she might play along, and the
thought made Max go crazy.
"NO!" he'd insisted. "My games
are COMPLICATED, and you

aren't *smart enough.*"

Max wondered if that was why Mandy Beth was bugging him now. Here she was, hands on her hips, tap-tapping her foot, daring him to try to rhyme "marker."

"Let me check, Mangy Breath," Max said. From his group's supply bin, Max pulled out a blue marker and gave it to her. "I hope you don't need it to be DARKER." He puffed out his chest and smirked.

Mandy Beth grunted. She tried again.

"Thanks. I'll bring it back when I'm DONE."

Max pressed his lips together. What rhymes with "*done*"? This time it took a little longer to come up with a word.

"*Doesn't matter*," he said at last. "We've got another ONE."

Max went back to cutting out leaves. He started humming his leave-me-alone hum. Mandy Beth glared at him, but returned to her table, carrying a blue magic marker — one that she really did not need.

Chapter Five

Double Trouble

When the mid-morning bell rang, Max hurried to be the first one outside. Recess was a good time for using up some of his extra energy. To get a break from his game, he decided to stick to a simple plan:

STAY AWAY FROM EVERYONE.

Too bad the *Fernandez twins* nabbed him right by the back doors.

"Hey, Max," Luis said, tugging on the sleeve of Max's jacket. "C'mon with us. We're going to play Four Square."

"Four Square, Max!" said Jorge. "It'll be fun."

Max eyed his friends. Same black hair. Same glasses. Matching clothes. He had to laugh. They even talked alike. Whatever Luis said, Jorge repeated, like an echo in a canyon.

Echo?! Max's jaw dropped and his stomach did a sudden flip. As long as he hung around

the twins, he would have TWO
times the rhymes. Two, four,
six, yikes!

Now he was in

DOUBLE TROUBLE!

Max hopped from one foot
to the other in a panic. *He had
to think of something fast.*
Square, fun, square, fun —

"I see a *bear* so I better
run," he said, a little too
loudly.

Luis scrunched his face in surprise. But Jorge shot a look over to where Max was pointing as if there really was a bear. Other kids who'd overheard started laughing.

Max didn't care.

He broke away and ran to the end of the schoolyard. At the wire fence, he bent over trying to catch his breath. The Fernandez twins had almost tripped him up. What a close call!

"Wow, Max. You're pretty far from the playground."

Max jumped. He had not heard Mandy Beth follow him.

Here I go again. "Gee . . . it's because I don't want YOU around," he snickered.

She scowled at him. "I know what you're doing. And it's not very funny."

Without skipping a beat, Max made a quick rhyme. "Why don't you give me all of your money?"

Mandy Beth clenched her teeth. "You'll be sorry if you don't let me play, too," she warned.

For a second, Max hesitated.

Mandy Beth would make his life miserable. But he couldn't help himself — he was on a roll. "No way, Mandy Beth. You're too dumb . . . And you smell like poo!" Then he gave a loud snort and took off again across the field.

"This is war, Maximus Todd!" she yelled after him. "THIS . . . IS . . . WAR!"

Max's voice faded in the distance. **"MORE! DOOR! CANDY STORE!"**

Chapter Six

A Near Miss

"Okay, class," announced Ms. Rudy after the break, "time to pair up with your reading buddy. Make sure to get your novel from the bins at the back. We'll start in three minutes."

Max's reading partner was Dana Daminski — funny Dana, smart Dana, Dana who smelled

like flowers and marshmallows.
Each time they sat beside
each other, Max felt like he
was floating with the clouds.

Even his Super Fidgets had no chance next to her. Dana did not seem to notice.

"Can you move our desks together while I go get the book?" she asked him.

Max nodded. It was hard to talk to Dana,

especially when he was floating.

He dragged over one desk. After that, the other. He pulled them until they lined up perfectly perfect. Then he went to get the chairs.

Only when Dana was coming back with their novel did Max

have the sense *he'd forgotten
something*. He shook his head.
Somehow it was important.
What could it be?

It came to him suddenly.

He HaDn'T RHYmeD!

In a flurry, Max thought back.

*There was something about
desks . . . and moving . . . and
flowers. No, no, no!*

*Something about getting a
book.*

Book! THAT was it!

"I put our desks together
Dana. *Look*." Max gave Dana a
dopey kind of smile, and then
started to get that floating
feeling again.

It didn't last long.

"Hey Max, do you remember what page we're ON?" an annoying voice called to him from across the classroom.

Humph, Max grumped. *Will she never quit?*

"BE GONE," HE WHISPERED FIERCELY.

"Mandy Beth, is there a problem?" asked Ms. Rudy.

"No, Ms. Rudy," Mandy Beth said. "I was seeing if Max remembered what page we got to last week."

"Fine, though you should

not speak so loudly in class."
Turning toward Max, Ms. Rudy
asked, "Do you remember
where we left off at?"

Max gaped at Ms. Rudy. Of
course he remembered. In fact,

Dana was pointing at the page
number for him.

BUT HE COULDN'T
SAY IT. NOT WITHOUT
a RHYme.

From the corner of his eye
he saw Mandy Beth covering
her mouth. She was trying hard
not to laugh.

At, cat, flat, sat . . . Nothing
worked.

At once, a terrible picture
filled Max's head. At the end

of his driveway was a big box
marked "FREE." Inside were
all his comic books. Hundreds
of kids lined the sidewalk and
street. They each grabbed a
comic, as they passed.

AND EVERY ONE OF THEM THREW AWAY THE PLASTIC BAGGY.

"It was forty-eight, Ms.
Rudy," Max said at last, when
Ms. Rudy looked like she was
going to ask someone else.
Everyone opened their books.
*Only Mandy Beth waited, her
eyebrows raised.*

"Imagine *th-that!*" stuttered Max.

Ms. Rudy peered at him. It felt to Max like she could see right into his thoughts. "Yes, Max," she said. "It *is* quite amazing that we've covered so many . . . pages."

"WELL, WE HAVE BEEN READING FOR AGES,"

Max added. Then he dropped his head deep into his book hoping that Ms. Rudy would say nothing more to him.

Chapter Seven

Clomp, Squeak

The early afternoon went much like the morning. Though he had to be careful of Mandy Beth, Max continued to rhyme. Every sentence. Every last word. And like he'd hoped, the game used up all his extra energy.

NO MORE SUPER FIDGETS!

Partway through Geography, Max got a funny feeling. He stopped labelling his map and glanced up. There was Mandy Beth! AGAIN. *She was weaving in and out between the rows, tracing a path to his desk.*

SHe LOOKeD LiKe a SNeaKY, SLiTHeRiNG SNaKe.

Max raised his hand right away. "Excuse me, Ms. Rudy."

Ms. Rudy had been grading projects. When she lifted her head, Mandy Beth spun around and walked over to the pencil sharpener.

"Yes, Max, what can I do for you?"

Ms. Rudy had ended her question with the word *you*. That was an easy word to rhyme.

"May I go to the washroom and get a drink, *too*?" he asked.

The teacher nodded and held out the washroom permission

tag. It was a card with a picture
of a toilet. Carrying the card
always embarrassed Max. Even
so, he waved it like a trophy at

Mandy Beth, who was pretending
to sharpen her pencil. She stuck
out her tongue.

Once he got into the hall,
Max let out a laugh. It was kind
of fun dodging bug-eyed Mandy
Beth. And now, because of her,
he had a little break from class.

Max decided to take his time.

He stopped and got a
drink at the fountain. He
peeked through the doors of
the classrooms he passed.
He walked sideways, then
backwards and then hopped on
one foot. Just for fun.

Clomp, squeak.
Clomp,
squeak.

Max
froze.

There was no mistaking the sound of shoes on a waxy school floor. Too bad they weren't his! Someone was coming from around the corner. Someone who might have something to say.

TO HIM.

Quickly, he twirled around to look at a poster hanging on the side wall.

Do you like dressing up? Strut your stuff at the school fashion show and help raise money for the food bank.

Maybe the someone would
go by without talking to him.
Maybe Max wouldn't be noticed
at all.

Clomp, squeak. Clomp,
squeak. The footsteps were
getting closer and closer.

Max Leaned Toward the Poster and Shut His Eyes.

The clomp-squeak stopped.

"Hey! How you doin' Maximus Todd?"

It was a kid's voice. But Max's heart pounded so loudly in his ears, he couldn't tell who.

Todd — odd, nod . . . He had a simple last name, but he needed time to think of a rhyme.

"I'm," Max began to say as he slowly turned. *Todd — clod, applaud.*

"Pretty," he continued,

trying to buy more time. *Todd
— thawed, pea pod.* He was
almost facing the kid now.

"*Good.*" *Todd — shod, police
squad.* Why aren't the words
working? He felt pinned like a
worm on a hook.

Max finally looked up to see
who was talking to him. Might
as well face the enemy.

It was Rod Vanslo, from the
fourth grade class! *Todd —
Rod.*

"ROD!" Max finished.

Rod gave him a nod and
continued down the hallway.
Max clutched his chest and

swallowed hard. He'd gotten a
break on his break!

WHaT a MiRacLe.

Figuring it was best not
to push his luck, Max made
a U-turn and hurried back to
class. He *didn't even bother to
stop at the washroom.*

Chapter Eight

Caught

"The leaves of the Venus Flytrap open wide, waiting for a visit from a tasty insect . . ."

It was late afternoon. And like Mandy Beth had said, Ms. Rudy was showing the class a video about plants (not ants). Everyone was interested and quiet.

Max was glad to simply sit
and let his mind drift while
the movie played. *It was
tough speaking in rhyme all
the time,* even if it kept him
focused.

On the screen, a rainbow
arched above a forest. From
three rows ahead, *Mandy
Beth suddenly turned and
sneered at
Max. He
wondered
why. Is
she still
thinking
of ways to
make me*

bumble and fumble and totally mess up on my game? **The thought gave him the heebie-jeebies.**

"Students," called Ms. Rudy from the front of the room, "you worked well today. As a reward you may spend our last half hour exploring a learning centre of your choice."

The class cheered. Everyone rushed at once to the different centres set up at the back of the room.

Max usually visited the building table. *But he saw that Mandy Beth was going there.* He decided to do some art instead.

While setting up his easel, someone tapped him on the shoulder. It was Mandy Beth. She moved in close. "Hi, Max," she said. "I see you are going to do some painting, like me."

Max backed away. *His arm hairs stood on end.*

"Yup. Now let me be," he rhymed.

Mandy Beth's mouth stretched out, *wide and mean.* "Fine. I was only wondering if you have any

orange?"

Chapter Nine

What Rhymes with Orange?!

Time stopped. Max's breath stuck in the back of his throat and his eyes grew large like two giant gumballs.

ORANGE! WHAT RHYMES WITH ORANGE?

What *rhymes with orange?* Max repeated to himself. The answer kept coming back like a boomerang.

NOTHiNG! NOTHiNG RHymes WiTH ORaNGe!

Max was sure it was one of those words that poets tried not to use in their poems. Like hiccups or bamboozle. And if poets can't rhyme orange, how could he?

Blue — *stew, green* — *bean, yellow* — *mellow, pink* — *think.* Every colour in the rainbow had a rhyme. *Every colour except orange!*

It was so close to the end of the school day. *He'd almost won at his game. Now it looked like Mandy Beth was going to ruin it for him.*

My stupid Super Fidgets! Max fumed. *Did I have to go and bet my comic books? Why can't I be like other kids and just sit still?*

He hung his head.

"Mandy Beth, do you

need some help?" It was their teacher.

"No, Ms. Rudy. I was checking if Max had any orange." Mandy

Beth explained it so sweetly, like she wasn't at all trying to wreck his life.

"Oh, I see," Ms. Rudy said.

She looked down at Max's paint tray.

"Mandy Beth, Max has three shades of green paint at his easel. No orange."

She paused.

"LOOKS TO ME LIKE MAX IS PLANNING TO PAINT SOME SPORANGE."

Chapter Ten

King of Rhyme

"Sporange?!" croaked Mandy Beth.

"Why yes," replied Ms. Rudy. "You know — from the video. Weren't you paying attention, Mandy Beth?"

Max wished he could blurt out, *"No she wasn't! She was too busy trying to make me lose my game!"*

"It's what scientists call the part of a plant that sends out spores to make more plants." Ms. Rudy looked at Max and continued. "Sporange is found on ferns."

SPORANGE! SPORANGE RHYMES WITH ORANGE!

A thousand fireworks
seemed to burst in Max's head.
He wanted to shout "WOOHOO"
and do cartwheels around the
room. *He had his rhyme! The*
game was not lost after all.

"I'll go get Mandy Beth the
orange now, Ms. Rudy," he

offered, showing her a wide grin. "If I need it, too, we can take turns."

MS. RUDY SMILED BACK. THERE WAS A STRANGE TWINKLE IN HER EYE.

Did she know all along about my secret game? Max wondered as the teacher walked away.

Max turned to hand Mandy Beth the jar of orange paint from the shelf. She hadn't moved the whole time. Only her mouth kept opening and closing — making a weird glug-glug sound.

"Here," he said. "Here's your orange, Mangy Breath. I probably won't be using it because I'm painting

SPORANGE."

Mandy Beth broke out of her trance. She yanked the jar from Max's hand. He thought she was going to explode.

But she didn't.

Instead, she threw her hands up in the air. "All right, all right. I give up, Max.

YOU WIN!

I won't make you rhyme anymore." Her arms flopped back to her sides.

Max squinted at her. "Good," he said. "Glad that's over . . . Sometimes I *snore*."

"Okay, Max. I get it. You are

the King of Rhyme."

"Yes I am!" he agreed,
raising his brush like a sceptre.
He opened one of the jars.
"Hey, this looks like . . .
slime."

Max laughed. Mandy Beth
couldn't help giggling, either.

"Well, I better go paint now,

Max," Mandy Beth said once they'd both settled down. "I just have one last question. Can I still walk home with you after school?"

Max thought hard. *Mandy Beth was as pesky as a swarm of mosquitoes. Yet she had helped him, in a way. Her tricks had kept him on his toes, making his Super Fidgets not so fidgety.*

"Fine. Just don't *drool*."

"Geesh!" Mandy Beth rolled her eyes.

"ENOUGH ALREADY!"

"I love *spaghetti*."

* * *

"Anything happen at school today?" asked Granpops. He was making Max's after-school snack: cheese cubes and crackers. Sarah sat in her high chair, trying to feed herself applesauce.

"Well, I did this painting." He pulled his artwork carefully out of his backpack.

"Nice," Granpops said. "Should get a spot on the fridge . . . Um. It's a plant, right?"

"YEAH, GRANPOPS. A FERN.

A LEAN, MEAN, GREEN FERN,"

said Max proudly. He hung his painting with some magnets and then stood back to admire it.

"I call it: A Rhyme for Orange."